Gerald the gerbil belonged
to Tom and Lucy.

"Will he be bored while we're at school?" asked Lucy.

Gerald's Busy Day

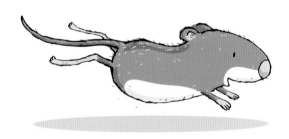

by Lynne Benton and Mark Marshall

FRANKLIN WATTS
LONDON•SYDNEY

First published in 2015 by
Franklin Watts
338 Euston Road
London
NW1 3BH

Franklin Watts Australia
Level 17/207 Kent Street
Sydney
NSW 2000

Text © Lynne Benton 2015
Illustration © Mark Marshall 2015

FSC
www.fsc.org
MIX
Paper from
responsible sources
FSC® C104740

A CIP catalogue record for this book is available
from the British Library.

ISBN 978 1 4451 3934 0 (hbk)
ISBN 978 1 4451 3939 5 (pbk)
ISBN 978 1 4451 3938 8 (library ebook)
ISBN 978 1 4451 3935 7 (ebook)

Series Editor: Jackie Hamley
Series Advisor: Catherine Glavina
Series Designer: Peter Scoulding

Printed in China

Franklin Watts is a divison of
Hachette Children's Books,
an Hachette UK company.
www.hachette.co.uk

"No," said Mum. "Gerbils sleep all day."

When they left, Gerald opened his cage door ...

and climbed out.

He ran across the floor ...

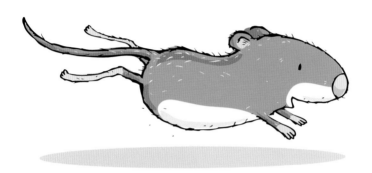

and up the curtain.

He jumped out of the window and on to the tree. Gerald ran down the tree ...

across the garden ...

and out of the gate!

He saw a window cleaner. Gerald ran under the ladder.

"Hey!" shouted the
window cleaner.
Gerald ran on.

He saw a balloon-seller.
Gerald ran past her.

"Hey!" shouted
the balloon-seller.
Gerald ran on.

He ran across the road, between all the cars.

"Hey!" the drivers shouted.
But Gerald ran on.

He ran round the corner,
then stopped. He saw a
big black cat.

"Oh goody, dinner!" said
the cat.

Gerald turned and ran
back round the corner ...

across the road.

He ran past the
balloon-seller ...

and under the ladder.

He ran in through the
gate, across the garden ...

and up the tree!

He jumped across to
the window ...

and climbed back into
his cage.

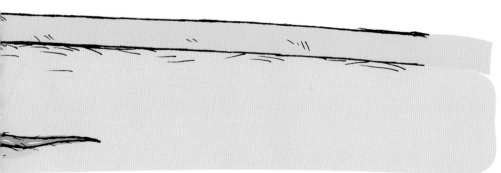

Soon Mum, Tom and Lucy came home. "He's still asleep," said Tom.

"I said he'd sleep all day!"
said Mum.

Puzzle 1

Put these pictures in the correct order.
Now tell the story in your own words.
Can you think of a different ending?

Puzzle 2

playful   energetic

drowsy

tired   lively

sleepy

Choose the words which best describe Gerald at the beginning and end of the story. Can you think of any more?

Answers

Puzzle 1

The correct order is:

1d, 2a, 3b, 4f, 5c, 6e

Puzzle 2

Gerald at the beginning – the correct words are energetic, playful. The incorrect word is drowsy. Gerald at the end – the correct words are sleepy, tired. The incorrect word is lively.

Look out for more stories:

Mary and the Fairy
ISBN 978 0 7496 9142 4

The Bossy Cockerel
ISBN 978 0 7496 9141 7

Tim's Tent
ISBN 978 0 7496 7801 2

Sticky Vickie
ISBN 978 0 7496 7986 6

Handyman Doug
ISBN 978 0 7496 7987 3

Billy and the Wizard
ISBN 978 0 7496 7985 9

Sam's Spots
ISBN 978 0 7496 7984 2

Bill's Scary Backpack
ISBN 978 0 7496 9468 5

Bill's Silly Hat
ISBN 978 1 4451 1617 4

Little Joe's Boat Race
ISBN 978 0 7496 9467 8

Little Joe's Horse Race
ISBN 978 1 4451 1619 8

Felix and the Kitten
ISBN 978 0 7496 7988 0

Felix, Puss in Boots
ISBN 978 1 4451 1621 1

Cheeky Monkey's Big Race
ISBN 978 1 4451 1618 1

The Naughty Puppy
ISBN 978 0 7496 9145 5

Prickly Ballroom
ISBN 978 0 7496 9475 3

The Animals' Football Cup
ISBN 978 0 7496 9477 7

The Animals' Football Camp
ISBN 978 1 4451 1616 7

That Noise!
ISBN 978 0 7496 9479 1

The Wrong House
ISBN 978 0 7496 9480 7

The Frog Prince and the Kitten
ISBN 978 1 4451 1620 4

For details of all our titles go to: www.franklinwatts.co.uk